nickelodeon

Puppy Takes a Bath

by Christine Ricci
illustrated by Tom Mangano

Ready-to-Read

Simon Spotlight

New York   London   Toronto   Sydney   New Delhi

Based on the TV series *Dora the Explorer*™ as seen on Nick Jr.™

SIMON SPOTLIGHT/NICKELODEON
An imprint of Simon & Schuster Children's Publishing Division
1230 Avenue of the Americas, New York, New York 10020
© 2006 Viacom International Inc. All rights reserved. NICKELODEON,
NICK JR., *Dora the Explorer,* and all related titles, logos, and characters are trademarks
of Viacom International Inc. All rights reserved, including the right of reproduction
in whole or in part in any form. SIMON SPOTLIGHT, READY-TO-READ, and colophon are
registered trademarks of Simon & Schuster, Inc. For information about special discounts
for bulk purchases, please contact Simon & Schuster Special Sales at 1-866-506-1949 or
business@simonandschuster.com.
Manufactured in the United States of America 0412 LAK
This Simon Spotlight edition 2012
2 4 6 8 10 9 7 5 3
ISBN 978-1-4424-4698-4 (pbk)
ISBN 978-1-4424-4697-7 (hc)

Hi! I am Dora.

This is my puppy.

My puppy loves
to roll in the dirt.

My puppy needs a bath!

Here is a tub of water.

Backpack has the soap
and the towel.

Help me find them!

The bath is ready.

But where is my puppy?

Is my puppy

hiding in the bushes?

No! My puppy is not
in the bushes.

Is my puppy hiding
in the flowers?

No! My puppy is not

in the flowers.

Is my puppy hiding
in the doghouse?

No! My puppy is not
in the doghouse.

I have an idea!

Here is a bone.

Here is my puppy!

My puppy sees the bone.

My puppy likes his bath.

My puppy is all clean!